Library and Archives Canada Cataloguing in Publication

McClintock, Norah
Masked / written by Norah McClintock.
(Orca soundings)

Issued also in an electronic format.
ISBN 978-1-55469-365-8 (bound).--ISBN 978-1-55469-364-1 (pbk.)

I. Title. II. Series: Orca soundings
PS8575.C62M38 2010 JC813'.54 C2010-903619-0

First published in the United States, 2010
Library of Congress Control Number: 2010929070

Summary: Rosie walks in on an armed robbery in her father's convenience store. Who is the masked man? And why is that loser from school there?

Orca Book Publishers is dedicated to preserving the environment and has printed this book on paper certified by the Forest Stewardship Council.

Orca Book Publishers gratefully acknowledges the support for its publishing programs provided by the following agencies: the Government of Canada through the Canada Book Fund and the Canada Council for the Arts, and the Province of British Columbia through the BC Arts Council and the Book Publishing Tax Credit.

Cover design by Teresa Bubela
Cover photography by Getty Images

ORCA BOOK PUBLISHERS
PO Box 5626, Stn. B
Victoria, BC Canada
V8R 6S4

ORCA BOOK PUBLISHERS
PO Box 468
Custer, WA USA
98240-0468

www.orcabook.com
Printed and bound in Canada.

13 12 11 10 • 4 3 2 1

To Li-Hsien, to whom I owe more than I can ever repay.

Chapter One

Daniel

"Uh, do you have a bathroom I can use?" I'm ready with an excuse for when the man behind the counter says no. I thought long and hard to come up with it. You have to when you're asking to use the bathroom in a convenience store, which doesn't have to provide one the way restaurants do. I have to get yes for an answer if my mission is going to be a success.

The man behind the counter scowls. He peers at me from under gray eyebrows that look like steel wool. Is he on to me? Does he suspect?

"What about your coffee and taquito?" he says. "Are you still going to want those?"

"Yeah. And a two-liter cola and the latest *Wrestling World*, if you have it." I throw those in to improve my chances of getting a yes.

"We have it. What about *Wresting Today*? You want that too?" His piggy little eyes drill into me. I see immediately where he's going. If I want to use the facilities, I'm going to have to cough up some more money. I take another glance at the magazine rack.

"And *Wrestling Connoisseur*," I say. What the heck—I'm getting paid enough. A few magazines aren't going to make a dent in my paycheck.

"Through the door beside the coolers and down one flight," the man behind the counter says.

As I head down the narrow aisle toward the coolers, I glance in the security mirror at the back of the store. The man at the counter, the owner, is watching me.

Going through the door beside the big Coke-sponsored cooler is like stepping from Oz back into Kansas. The tile floor in the store sparkles. The wooden floor on the other side of the door is dingy, scuffed and slightly warped. The lights in the store are blindingly bright. On the other side of the door there is only a single naked lightbulb that makes the places it doesn't hit look inky and a little spooky. The walls of the store are chockablock with neatly displayed and colorful products. The walls of the small room are bare except for a car dealership calendar that hangs from a nail directly above a battered old table and chair. On the table is an adding machine—I didn't even know those still existed. Next to it is a two-drawer olive-green filing cabinet. On the wall, in an ancient fixture with a pull chain, is another naked lightbulb. This is where the store owner does his accounts. To the left of the door is a flight of wooden stairs. But I don't go down it.

Instead, I listen. It's quiet in here. It's also quiet out in the store. I tiptoe over to the desk. I'd been expecting a computer, but there isn't one. I open the top drawer of the filing cabinet. It's jammed with files. I thumb through them, looking for the one I've been sent to find. I don't see it. I close that drawer, open the next one and thumb through more folders.

Bingo! There it is, neatly labeled.

I pull it out and scan the sheets inside. They look like the ones that were described to me. I dig the miniature camera—a spy camera, if you can believe it—out of my pocket and photograph every sheet. I put everything back into the folder and replace the folder in the file cabinet. I tuck the camera into my pocket. I start back to the door.

Before I get there, I hear the man behind the counter yell something—a name. I'm about to push the door open and go back into the store when I hear a different voice—a familiar one. I decide to wait. If I go out there, I'll be recognized. If I'm recognized, I'll be exposed. If I'm exposed, I'll have to abort my mission. And if I abort... let's just say I don't want to kiss my paycheck goodbye.

Chapter Two

Rosie

"What's taking so long?" Corey calls.

"*Shhhh!*" I dart out into the living room, my finger pressed against my lips, and glower at him. I must have told him a million times to be quiet. Shouting does not constitute being quiet. "If you have something to say, you have to come to where I am and say it."

Corey blinks at me. He's standing near the stereo, his head sideways as he reads the titles in my dad's CD collection. I don't know why he's bothering. They're almost all jazz, and as far as I know, Corey doesn't like jazz.

"I'll be ten minutes," I say. "Do you think you can keep quiet for ten minutes?"

"Sure. Whatever." He shrugs, like it's no big deal.

"My dad is right downstairs, Corey."

"So?" Another shrug. Suddenly I want to strangle him. "You said that once he goes downstairs, he's there until the store closes," Corey says. "You said he never comes back up here."

"Unless there's a reason. I said he doesn't come up unless there's a reason. If he hears shouting, that's a reason."

Corey looks irritated, and that scares me a little, so I dial it back. I don't want this to go wrong. I can't afford it to.

"Just ten more minutes, I promise," I say.

"You said you'd be ready when I got here," Corey complains. "I've been standing out here doing nothing ever since I arrived."

"I'm sorry. But it's all my dad's fault. He had a bunch of stuff he wanted me to do in the store." That's the number-two thing I'm not going to miss—that stupid store. The number-one thing is my dad. All he cares about is his store and his profit margin, which is why he watches kids and single moms like they're criminals who only come in to rip him off instead of customers he should be glad to have. It's why I never let my friends come near the place. If my dad treated any of them the way he treats other kids, it'd be all over school.

I run to Corey and kiss him on the cheek, hoping it will calm him down.

Hoping, too, that it will make him remember the good times we used to have and the good times that are ahead for us.

"I'll be ready before you know it," I say. I scurry back to my room and continue to stuff clothes into a green plastic garbage bag. The suitcase I planned to take is already full. So is my backpack. And I'm determined not to leave anything behind, even though I'm going to have to buy a lot of new clothes pretty soon.

I work as fast as I can, and not just because I promised Corey. I want to be gone in case Leon comes by. I tried to discourage him. I told him it wasn't a good idea, that my dad was in a bad mood, and he knows what that means. I told him that I had to work in the store, so there was no point in showing up. Usually he does exactly what I tell him, but today I'm not so sure. There was something different in his voice when he called. There was something different in his face all day at school too. But he wouldn't tell me what the matter was.

So, fine, let him come even after I told him not to. Let him ring the bell in the back and get no answer. There's no way he'll dare go into the store to see if I'm there. There's no way he'll ask my dad where I am. Neither of them will know I'm gone until it's too late.

I jam the last sweater from the bottom drawer of my dresser into the bag and close it with a twist tie. There. Done.

I pick up the bag and the suitcase, sling the strap of my backpack over my shoulder and drag everything down the hall to the living room. That's when I hear it.

"Rosie!"

My dad's voice rises through the floor like he's holding a bullhorn and has pressed it right up against the ceiling of the store.

"Rose, get down here! Now!"

Corey looks at me, annoyed, and waits to see what I'm going to do.

"I have to go down there," I say. "If I don't, he'll come up here."

"So? You think I'm afraid of your old man? You think I'd be here if I was?"

"He probably just needs me to find something. I'll be right back."

Corey scowls. He's been in a sour mood ever since he walked through the door, even though he wasn't in a sour mood last night. This isn't going at all the way I imagined it.

"I'll be as quick as I can."

I slip out the door that leads from the kitchen into the hall and run down the stairs. When I slip into the store, I lock the door behind me. I don't want to take the chance that Corey will decide to come down. I hope I'm right about my dad. I hope he just needs to ask me something and that he hadn't heard Corey's voice. I also hope that Leon hasn't shown up.

Chapter Three

Daniel

When the old man calls her name, which I hear as a rumble from behind the door, I think that Rosie is probably his wife. A lot of these places make it because the husband and wife both work there. The kids, too, as soon as they're old enough. The money stays in the family that way.

But just as I'm about to open the door and go back into the store, I hear her voice loud and clear: "What's up, Dad? I was just about to take a shower, so..."

You don't mistake a voice like that—kind of husky, low for a girl, but not old-lady low. Smoky low. Sexy low. There are a lot of guys at school who are crazy about that voice.

Rosie's voice. Rosie Mirelli.

She's in my history class.

The old man called her, and she called him Dad. What do you know? The princess is no princess after all, not if her dad owns this place.

Part of me thinks she'll never recognize me. She never looks at me at school. She treats me like a ghost, like someone who inhabits a whole different world from hers. A world of shadows and darkness, not a Rosie world filled with bright colors.

Then again, she's just the kind of girl who, if she were to see me trespassing in her world, would say, "What do you think you're doing here?" Not that that would be a big deal ordinarily. I bet I'm not the first kid from school to come in here. It would mean nothing—except for one thing. Except for Leon.

Leon lives next door to me. His mom and my mom talk all the time. Mostly they talk about their kids, about Leon and his brothers, about me and my sister. And because of all that talk, Leon knows about my job. I'm a mystery shopper. That's someone who is hired to go into a store or a restaurant like an ordinary customer but who checks on the service and whatever else he's hired to check on. All kinds of people are mystery shoppers—old people, young people, kids like me. Ordinary people. People you'd never suspect. My uncle got me the job. He knows a guy who runs a mystery-shopper business. But that's not why I'm in the store today. Today my mission is different.

I'm here because I was hired by a friend of my uncle's who's a real-estate developer. A Donald Trump wannabe. He has quietly bought up a lot of property in the area, and to complete his deal, he needs to buy this store. But the owner—Rosie's dad—won't sell. So my uncle's friend hired me to take a look at Mr. Mirelli's finances. That way, he says, he can come up with the right price and maybe the right pressure to motivate him to sell. I don't understand the whole thing. All I know is that I'm being well paid—if I succeed.

Leon asked me about my job one time. And he teases me about it at school sometimes, calling me Mystery Man. He's said it a couple of times when he was with Rosie. And I bet he explained to Rosie what he meant. So I bet she'll say something to her dad if I suddenly appear through a door that leads to a bathroom that her father doesn't usually let customers use. And then he'll know there's some other reason for me to be there, because mystery shoppers are hired by companies that want to check on their employees. Rosie's father doesn't have any employees. He'll know he didn't hire me. He might figure out what I was doing back here, and then what?

I hang back and wait.

"Where did you put the order book when you finished with it?" Mr. Mirelli says.

There's a moment of silence and then a slapping sound, like a teacher makes when he slaps an exercise book down onto your desk.

"Did you even look?" Rosie says, using that same snotty tone on her dad that she uses on people she thinks are beneath her at school, acting all the time like her dad owns a Walmart instead of a crummy little convenience store, like she's some kind of big deal.

Her dad doesn't yell back at her though. All he says is, "What about the beans? That guy who always comes in for beans couldn't find the kind he likes and neither could I."

"I rearranged that aisle, Daddy. Remember?" She says it like she's talking to a four-year-old.

"Well, go and grab me a couple of cans, will you? I told him if he came back, I'd have some waiting for him. Then you can take your shower."

Silence. I figure she must be doing what her dad told her. In another minute she'll be gone, and I can get on with my assignment. I'll be in the clear.

I hear footsteps coming toward me. It's probably Rosie, going to get the beans her dad asked for.

The footsteps stop right outside the door to the basement. I hold my breath, while at the same time telling myself

I'm acting stupid. There's nothing back here but a cramped little office and a flight of stairs. She has no reason to come back here.

The doorknob turns.

I look for a place to hide and consider diving down the stairs.

The door swings open.

I gasp.

"There you are," Mr. Mirelli says, scowling at me. I begin to wonder whether he's capable of any other expression. "I thought maybe you'd fallen in."

I force myself to laugh at his feeble joke. Then I think, maybe he doesn't mean it as a joke. Maybe he suspects something. He peers around me, scanning the bare little office like he's checking to make sure everything is still there. I try to stay calm. I try not to look guilty. I tell myself there's no way he could ever know what I did in here and no way he'll ever find out. I also wonder if what I did is a crime.

"Well, come on," he says gruffly.

I step out and look around for Rosie. I don't see her anywhere. She must have gone upstairs already to have her shower.

"I've got your stuff up front," Mr. Mirelli says. "Assuming you still want it."

"Yeah, I still want it."

A bell jangles. It's the bell above the store's front door. The old man and I both turn. When I see what's coming through that door, I want to bolt back into the little office, slam the door, lock it and hide out in the basement. It's possible Mr. Mirelli feels the same way, but he doesn't move. Neither of us do.

Chapter Four

The Masked Man

I swear I can see myself, as if I'm watching me on TV or in a movie. I've seen scenes like it a million times in a million cop shows. A guy is about to walk into a store. But first he pulls a mask down over his face, and in that split second, as the mask or the balaclava or whatever comes down to cover him, you see that he's sweating. You see his hands are shaking too. You think maybe he's a junkie, maybe that's where the shakes come from. For sure you know he's desperate. Why else would he be about to stick up a convenience store? I mean, how much could there be in the cash drawer, especially when so many people use debit cards? So, yeah, he must be desperate.

And nervous, just like I am when I pull the balaclava down over my head.

Nervous? Make that scared to death, because once you enter a store with the intent to commit a robbery, you're on the wrong side of the law. And once you're on the wrong side, anything can happen. For example, the guy behind the cash register could have a gun and he could reach for it, even if you tell him *you* have a gun, even if you wave your gun in his face. Some store owners are like that. They're cowboys.

They don't like to be pushed around. Or maybe they've been robbed before—maybe they've been robbed one time too often—and now here you are, and the man behind the cash means to make you pay for all those other robberies. So maybe he shoots. Or maybe he tries to shoot, but you shoot first. In your mind, it's self-defense. In the law's mind, it's assault while committing a robbery. If the guy dies, it's murder. Either way, if they catch you, you're in bigger trouble than you bargained for.

Or maybe the guy behind the cash register has an alarm system and he trips it, and the cops show up. Maybe one of the cops is a rookie. Maybe he's over-eager. Maybe this is the chance he's been waiting for all his life. He's been waiting to take out a bad guy. Maybe he's so excited that he forgets he's supposed to issue a warning. Maybe he just decides to pull the trigger and make his dream come true.

All those thoughts jangle in my head as I open the door and cross from the street into the store. I even think to myself in that split second, It's not worth it. I should forget the whole thing and go home. The risk is too big.

But it's already too late.

I read somewhere that the army figured out back in World War II that soldiers who suffer from post-traumatic stress disorder aren't cowards. They used to think they were. They used to put guns in soldiers' hands and tell them to kill, *kill*, ***kill***, and then think there was something wrong with them if they fell apart after they'd obeyed the order. They used to think that real soldiers did what they were told, so if you told them to kill the enemy, they did it, and that was that. It was all okay.

But it wasn't all okay. Guys fell apart. They got screwed up. Until some genius figured out that most regular people get messed up when they kill other people. They get even more messed up when they spend months and years killing people. Apparently getting messed up after killing people is normal. Getting used to killing people—*that's* screwed up.

So then the army changed the way it trained soldiers. They stopped talking about killing people. Instead, they talked about *securing targets*, like securing didn't mean killing, even though it really did, and targets didn't mean people, even though it really did. In other words, they made it impersonal.

And you know what?

They found that soldiers were a whole lot better at killing when they were ordered to secure a target instead of being told to kill people, even if those people were the enemy.

I know. You're wondering: What do soldiers have to do with a masked man?

Well, you can learn lessons from all kinds of places, even from the army. A person who is, say, scared to death about something he's doing can decide to keep it impersonal. It's a mind game, like how they tell people who are afraid of public speaking to imagine that the whole audience is sitting out there in their underwear. How can you be afraid of a whole bunch of people in their underwear, right? You could be creeped out. But intimidated? No way.

A guy—like, for instance, me—who is going into a new situation can learn from that too. For example, I can walk into that store and tell myself that the owner is just a useless old man. He's powerless too, because, well, who has the gun? I can think of the store as my target. I can think of my mission as securing the target. I can even pretend it's a game: I'm a character in a game. I have an objective. The clock is running, and I am going to *win*.

So there I am in the store. The mask is down over my face, and my hand is coming out of my coat pocket, wrapped around a gun. The store owner, partway back along one wall, is staring at me, his mouth hanging open like he's trying to figure out if this is a joke or if it's for real. But there's someone else with the owner. A guy. Is he a customer? Maybe not. No, definitely not. And, at the far side of the store, just for a second, the top of her head visible before she drops down behind an aisle of shelves, there's a girl. She's probably hoping I haven't seen her. Then, like a flash from the sky aimed right at the center of my forehead, comes a blinding thought:

What if she has a cell phone? What if she's dialing 9-1-1?

I start to think that maybe what I'm doing isn't such a great idea. I'm thinking it's getting too complicated. There are so many things I haven't considered, so many things that don't feature in my plan.

But I've already crossed the line. I'm in the store with a gun.

I tell myself that my plan is a good one. I tell myself I'm not going to back down now.

"This is a stickup," I say.

Chapter Five

Rosie

Not only are the beans exactly where I said they were, but they haven't hidden themselves in a cloak of invisibility since I put them there. They're right out in the open. You can't miss them. That tells me that my dad didn't even bother to look for them. No surprise there. It's always, "Rosie, where's the soup?

Rosie, where's that new shipment of disposable razors? Rosie, what did you do with the marshmallows?" A walk down this aisle or that one would answer those questions and a million other ones besides. But no, why take so much as a single step when you can just yell for Rosie? It's one more reason I'm glad Corey came back and is waiting for me upstairs.

I stand up, holding the beans, my mouth open and ready to yell at my dad while I wave the cans at him. I see my dad with a boy I recognize from school, a dork named Daniel. Where did he come from? I see that my dad is staring at something. I turn my head.

There's a masked man in the store, and it isn't Halloween.

I duck down again—fast.

I hear someone say, "This is a stickup." It's the guy in the mask. He has a weird voice, like it's not his normal voice. He says, "Is there anyone else in the store?"

That tells me that the masked man hasn't seen me.

"No," my dad says without even a second's hesitation.

The masked man doesn't know I'm there—for all the good it does. My cell phone is upstairs. There's a phone in the store, but it's behind the counter. I'd have to get past the masked man to reach it—or to get to the door to the upstairs apartment or the one to the street. I'm stuck in the canned food aisle. There's nothing I can do. Unless...

I'm still clutching a can of beans in each hand. The cans have the heft of rocks. What if I sneak up behind the masked man? What if I smash one of those cans onto the back of his head? Maybe it wouldn't knock him out, but it would distract him for long enough that my dad could do something.

"I already told you," my dad says. "There's no one else in the store." There's a panicky edge to his voice.

I wish I could take another look at what's happening. But what if I get caught? No, I have to stay hidden. That's the best thing to do. Let the masked man take whatever he wants. Then he'll go away. No one will get hurt. My dad will call the police—and that will be good. While he's busy with them, I can make my getaway. I start very slowly to crawl down the aisle toward the back of the store. There are cases of pop stacked there. I can hide behind them until it's all over.

I'm barely breathing.

I maneuver around the spot where the floor squeaks. I've asked my dad a million times to fix it, but he always says no. He says he likes to know when there's someone in the aisle farthest from the cash. He says that squeak lets customers know that he knows they're there.

I'm almost at the end of the aisle. There's a gap of a couple of feet between it and the cases of pop. I'll have to cross it bcfore I can hide. I draw in a deep breath as I get ready. I pray I won't be seen. I'm just about to dart across the gap when a pair of legs blocks me.

I look up—and see two eyes through the eyeholes in the mask. I also see a gun in a gloved hand.

"Well, well," the masked man says in a deep voice. A second gloved hand reaches down and yanks me to my feet. My father is staring at me. His face is pale.

"Rosie," he gasps. He turns to the masked man. "Please don't hurt my daughter. Take anything you want, but don't hurt her."

The masked man shoves me in front of him as he advances toward my father. A funny thing—his grip isn't nearly as hard as his voice.

Chapter Six

Daniel

A gun.

The guy has a gun. I'm smack in the middle of a real-life armed robbery. The guy in the mask must be on drugs or something. He must be desperate. Why else would he be robbing a convenience store? My uncle's friend isn't paying me enough for this.

We've got our hands up—Mr. Mirelli and me. I glance at the front of the store, specifically, at the door. At the lock on the door. As far as I can tell, it's in the unlocked position, which means anyone could walk in off the street. That would be fine if it turned out to be a couple of cops. But I don't see any cops out there—not that this is proof positive that there aren't any. There are so many posters, advertising everything from a new type of gum and a deal on calling cards to a muffin-and-coffee combo, which store owners agree to put up because they get paid to. With all those posters on the windows, it's impossible to see much of the street. It's also impossible for anyone on the street, like the cops, to get a good look at what's happening inside.

At first I think the guy is a total amateur for leaving the door unlocked. But he's obviously not a complete idiot.

Right away he asks if there's anyone else in the store, and he doesn't take Mr. Mirelli's word for it when he answers, "No." He checks it out for himself, waving the gun at us to show us he's not kidding. He keeps the gun on us while he checks the aisles. He still has it on us when he ducks down for an instant. When he straightens up—the gun hasn't wavered so much as a millimeter—he's got Rosie by the arm. Her face is white and her eyes are enormous and fixed on that gun. She's scared. Well, join the club.

The guy in the mask shoves her along in front of him. He points the gun at her.

"You try anything, and she gets it," he tells Mr. Mirelli. "You understand?"

Mr. Mirelli nods vigorously. He's like one of those bobble-head toys you see in the back of cars sometimes. He nods and nods and nods.

"You want cash?" he says to the guy in the mask. "You can have it. You can have all of it."

He has his own store, but I bet he's had experience as a store manager somewhere else because he sounds like he's read the company manual of one of the big chain stores. I've thumbed through a few of them myself, for my job. Some of the details in each one are different, but most of the big items are the same, especially when it comes to situations like these. In situations like these, no one is supposed to act like a hero. What they're supposed to do is hand over the cash, let the robber make his getaway, and then, when it's safe—and *only* when it's safe—call the cops. Nobody wants their store to be the place where some innocent customers get killed because a manager or employee decides to try to save the few hundred dollars that are in the cash drawer.

Mr. Mirelli nods toward the cash register. He's trying to speed things up. The faster the robber is out of the store, the less chance there is that anything will happen to Rosie.

"I'll open the register for you," Mr. Mirelli says to the robber. He raises his hands higher, a show of submission and good will. He even manages a shaky smile as he says, "We had a good day. It's all yours. Let me get it for you."

The guy in the mask doesn't answer right away. The only thing I can see are his eyes, so I focus in on them. I'm stunned when I see hesitation in them. Mr. Mirelli is offering to empty the cash register for the masked man, and the masked man is standing there holding on to Rosie and looking like he's actually thinking it over—should he go for it or not? I'm totally confused. He came in here with a mask and a gun. He announced it was a stickup. He used that actual word. So what's he thinking about?

Then he waves the gun at Mr. Mirelli and me, telling us, okay, yeah, he wants the cash, and he wants us to go on ahead of him. In the instant before Mr. Mirelli turns away from me, I see the relief on his face. I know what he's thinking. He's thinking, If I hand over the cash, the guy will go away. I'm thinking the same thing.

We march up to the front of the store, and I take a closer look at the lock on the door. The guy in the mask has left it open. He's also left the sign turned to *Open*. Anyone could walk in, and that makes me nervous. If you introduce an unexpected element into a drama like this, anything can happen.

"I'm going to go around behind the counter," Mr. Mirelli says. His hands are still up over his head. "Okay? Is that okay?"

The guy in the mask grunts and nods. He's still holding on to Rosie.

Mr. Mirelli starts to lower his hands and then thinks better of it. Up they go again.

"I'm going to have to put my hands down so I can get around there, okay?" he says. He nods at the hinged opening in the counter.

"Okay," the guy in the mask says in that weird voice of his. It's a put-on voice for sure. He's disguising his real voice just like he's disguising his face, which I think is odd—until I think about it again. Maybe he's from the neighborhood. Maybe he's been in this store before. Maybe he's been in here a million times. Maybe he thinks that if he uses his real voice, Mr. Mirelli will recognize it.

Mr. Mirelli lowers his hands slowly, like he's afraid that any sudden movement will provoke gunfire. He reaches for the hinged panel and lifts it. His eyes are on the man in the mask the whole time. He slips behind the counter and raises his hands again as he slides sideways toward the cash register.

"I'm going to put my hands down again," he says when he's finally positioned in front of the register. "To get the money." His hands creep down again and he reaches out to the register to key in the code that will let him open it.

I'm relieved. It's almost over.

Chapter Seven

The Masked Man

I can't breathe. The mask is sticking to my face. My clothes are sticking to my body. How does anyone ever pull off a job like this?

We're at the cash now, but it seems to have taken about an hour to get here. Any minute now the old man is going to give me the money, and then I can get out of here.

I don't like that there's another guy in the store. I still can't figure out where he came from. I didn't see him when I was outside. And I was careful. I looked. Even with all those posters, I looked. I checked. I double-checked. I walked into a situation that I thought I understood, and all of a sudden there's someone there that I hadn't counted on.

Not only that, but he keeps looking at me like he's some kind of expert on how all this is supposed to go down and he's checking to see if I'm doing it right. He's making me nervous—and I'm nervous enough as it is.

But it's going to be okay. It has to be okay. All I have to do is take the cash, then take some getaway insurance, and it's all over.

I'm holding on to the girl, Rosie. She hasn't said a word since I grabbed her. Maybe she's in shock. That can happen to people, especially when they see a gun pointed at them. They freeze up. Their systems start to shut down. That's another reason I need to get this over with and get out of here.

The old man is scared too, but he's trying not to show it. He's trying to take charge. I can see the sweat glistening on his forehead and on his upper lip, but still he's telling me what to do. I'm not surprised. Guys like him are used to being in charge. But he's also playing it smart—and safe. If he needs to put his hands down, he tells me ahead of time. He tells me exactly what he's going to do.

That's because of Rosie. He really seems worried about her, like he thinks I'm going to off her or something. Now *that* surprises me. It's not how I pictured him.

If you look at him or if you study him through the store window, you see he's always got a lemon-sucking look on his face. He glowers at every teenager who sets foot in the place. His eyes are on them the whole time they're in the store. Or they're on the security mirrors above the aisles that give him a good view of most of the place.

He's nicer to adults. He exchanges weather talk with some of the women and sports talk with some of the men. But he never cracks a smile. Never. And he watches them as closely as he watches the kids. He tries to pretend that he doesn't, but his eyes keep darting up to those mirrors. They're sharp and bright, like he's trained them to take in every detail of what goes down in the store.

The way he looks and the way he acts with his customers, that's the way I thought he would be with Rosie. I even thought maybe he'd give me trouble, you know, like, "Go ahead and shoot her if that's what you want to do, but I am not handing so much as one dime over to a punk like you."

I'm holding Rosie. I feel her tremble, and I'm sorry about that. I'm sorry I have to scare her. But there's no other way. I watch the old man lower his hands to the cash register. I wonder how much money is in there—not that it makes any difference. I try to ignore the other guy, the one I hadn't counted on. I try to pretend he isn't staring at me. I wish the old man would hurry up.

I can't breathe.

Chapter Eight

Rosie

I know it's stupid, but all I can think about is Corey. He's upstairs waiting for me. What if he gets impatient? What if he decides to come down here and see what's taking me so long? What if he startles the guy in the mask?

If only my father hadn't called for me. If only he had for once—just for once—left his precious cash register to look for those beans himself. But no. That would be like expecting a dog to pick up after itself. Instead, he did what he always does. He yelled for me.

In five minutes, it would have been a completely different story. I would have been gone. He could have shouted himself hoarse if he'd wanted to. I wouldn't have heard him. I would never hear him again.

But it wasn't five minutes later, so it didn't happen that way. He *did* call me. And because he's so impossible to live with, because he thinks he can control every second of every minute of my life, because I was afraid that he would come upstairs if I didn't answer, I came down here, like a servant running to do her master's bidding.

Oh god. Please don't let Corey come down here. Don't let him startle the guy in the mask. Open the cash drawer, Daddy. Open it and scoop out the cash.

Give it to the guy in the mask. Give him anything he wants. Make him go away. And when he does go, call the cops. Call them and tell them what happened. While you're busy with that, I can go.

But my dad doesn't hurry. He's moving slowly, like an old man whose arthritis is acting up. It's taking him forever to get up to the cash, forever to lower his hands, forever to start punching in his stupid security code.

There's also a part of me that wants to run. I could too. The guy in the mask is holding my arm, but he doesn't have a tight grip on it. I could pull free easily. I could run for the door. It's not locked. I checked. I could race out into the street and dive to the pavement at the right or the left of the door. He wouldn't be able to see me. Not with all those posters in the window. Every poster brings in a little extra money—money, money, money. That's what it's all about for my dad. That and how to make my life miserable.

But if I run, if I break free, the guy in the mask might shoot. Maybe he'll shoot me. Or maybe he'll shoot my dad. I think about that for a moment. I'm ashamed because I actually imagine it. There's only me and my dad now. If anything happens to him, I inherit everything. All the money he has tucked away will be mine.

I glance at my dad. My face is burning. He's opening the cash drawer. He's about to hand over all of the money inside to the guy in the mask. He actually offered it to the guy. He told him, Take anything you want in the place but please don't hurt my daughter. *Please*. Do you have any idea how often my dad says please? Maybe once in a decade, and never to me. But he said it just now, to the guy in the mask. If I didn't know any better, I'd say he doesn't want anything bad to happen to me. But if that's true, if he really cares about me, he wouldn't be trying to control me all the time. He would let me do what I want for a change.

The cash drawer is open, and my dad is emptying out the twenties. Then the tens. Then the fives. He glances at the guy in the mask. He told the guy he's had a good day in the store. He told him there's a lot of cash in the drawer. But it doesn't look to me like there are more than five or six twenties in there and an equal number of tens. There aren't many fives either. And if I notice that, then the guy in the mask must notice too. Maybe he's staring hard at my dad right now. Maybe that's why my dad is just standing there, a flimsy little stack of bills in his hand. He sighs. I hear him. Then he lifts the cash drawer and pulls out all the bills he keeps underneath—a bunch of twenties and some fifties. He puts them all in a neat stack and sets the bills on the counter.

"There," he says to the guy in the mask. "There's nearly a thousand dollars there. Take it. It's yours. Take it and leave my daughter. I won't call the police. I promise. Just leave my daughter."

The guy in the mask doesn't move.

Take it, I said in my head. Take it and go. And please don't let Corey come down here. Don't let him startle the guy in the mask.

The guy in the mask nudges me forward.

"Pick it up," he says in that weird, fake ultra-deep voice of his.

His grip tightens on me as I reach for the money. As soon as my hands close around it, he pulls me back.

"Hold it up," he says.

I hold up the money, and he takes it from my hand.

"Good. That's good," my father says, as if he's praising a child who has just finished brushing his teeth. "You can go now. We won't move. None of us will. I promise."

But the guy in the mask says, "She's coming with me."

Chapter Nine

Daniel

It's weird. I'm scared. I can tell because my shirt is wet under my arms and my mouth is dry. Also, I have this spaced-out feeling, as if what's happening is something I'm watching, not something I'm actually in the middle of. For the first little while, my eyes refuse to move from the gun. I've never seen a real one. For sure I've never seen one this close up, held by a jittery guy in a mask who means business. But that's only for a little while. Then that spaced-out feeling gets stronger. The stronger it gets, the less I look at the gun and the more I feel like I'm floating above the man in the mask, Rosie, her father, even myself, watching everything unfold. A crazy calm takes over. Yeah, it's weird.

I'm no expert. I've never been in a situation like this before. But if you ask me, the guy in the mask is an amateur. He seems to be letting Mr. Mirelli take the lead. Not that that doesn't mean we're all afraid. We are. I see Mr. Mirelli's hands shake when he takes the cash out of the drawer. Rosie's hands shake just like her old man's when she picks up the money like she's told and lets the guy in the mask snatch it from her.

More evidence that he's new at this: he didn't lock the door or put up the Closed sign. And now, instead of taking off with the money, he wants to take Rosie with him, which I'm sure the cops will see as kidnapping. A thousand bucks, and instead of being smart, he's making it even worse. If they catch him, he'll be locked up for a long time.

He says the girl is coming with him, and Mr. Mirelli and Rosie both say the same thing at the exact same time. They say, "No."

Mr. Mirelli doesn't want the man to take his daughter. He's actually saying no to a man who has a gun pointed at him. Even more surprising, Rosie says no to a man who has a good grip on her and who, if you ask me, can do pretty much whatever he wants.

Does the guy in the mask get angry? Does he threaten Mr. Mirelli and Rosie? Does he remind them that, in case they didn't notice, he has a gun?

No. Instead, he looks surprised, even with that mask over his face. It's his eyes that give him away. They pop open like kernels of popcorn.

"She's coming with me," he says again and stops abruptly because their response has surprised him so much that he's forgotten himself and has slipped into a normal voice. He sucks in a deep breath. He lowers his voice again to disguise it. "She's coming with me," he says for the third time.

I don't even notice what Rosie does after that. I don't look at her father either. I'm staring at the guy in the mask. I'm thinking about those four words that he said in his normal voice. I look him over, taking in every detail.

He's tall—much taller than Rosie, but not quite as tall as me. There's not a lot of meat on him. I'm slim, but I'm all muscle. Maybe he's all muscle too, but I'm willing to bet he's mostly string bean. Besides the mask, which is really one of those hats you can wear when you're skiing on a cold day and can pull down over your face so that the only things that show are your eyes through two eyeholes and your mouth through a mouth hole—besides that, he's wearing gloves, a long black coat like the guy in *The Matrix*, black jeans and black boots. The boots have worn-down heels and a triangle-shaped nick on the right instep.

They make me think of my next-door neighbor. He saved up for months to buy a pair of boots just like those. The second day he had them, one of his brothers, the younger one who, it turns out, wears the same size boots, borrowed them without asking and got into a fight while he was wearing them. When he returned them, they had a triangle-shaped nick on the right instep. The whole neighborhood heard the two of them going at it, with their mother in the middle, first yelling at them to stop and then begging them.

I stare at those boots and I wonder, What are the chances?

But I open my mouth anyway. I say, "Hey."

The guy in the mask turns toward me, which I guess is what Mr. Mirelli has been waiting for because the very second the guy turns his head, I see out of the corner of my eye Mr. Mirelli slipping his hand under the counter. I think he must have some kind of button down there that sets off an alarm. I figure he's pressing it. That's the only reason I say what I say next. I think that Mr. Mirelli has tripped the alarm and that the cops are getting the information that there's something going down in this store and any minute now they'll be on their way here. That's why I say what I say.

I say, "Leon?"

Chapter Ten

The Masked Man

I planned. I thought through all the angles. I knew down to the minute when I was going to walk through the door and exactly what I'd do once I was inside. When I found someone in there I hadn't counted on, I didn't let it throw me. I adapted. I kept going. After all, I walked in there as a man with a plan.

I was going to see it through no matter what. It was going to be easy—at least, it was the way I mapped it out. I'd wait until the old man and the girl were alone in the store. I'd go in. I'd wave the gun. I'd grab the girl. I'd go. Done.

There's this thing I heard one guy say to another guy in a movie once: *If it wasn't for bad luck, you'd have no luck at all.* That's how I feel when I'm surprised by someone in the store that I hadn't expected. But I roll with the punches. I work around him. I refuse to let him stop me from doing what I came in to do.

But my plan starts to unravel.

First, I take my eyes off the old man for a split second when the guy I hadn't counted on says, "Hey."

Then, by the time I turn back to the old man, I see him pulling his hand out from someplace under the counter.

At the exact moment I see what he's pulling out from under there—a gun—I hear the guy I hadn't counted on say, "Leon?"

I'm staring at that gun—that's something else I didn't plan for. I don't remember anyone saying anything about a gun. Then someone is saying my name—"Leon?"—as in, "Leon, is that you under that mask?" I feel Rosie's arm stiffen. I see her turn. I see that she's not scared anymore. I see that she's staring into my eyes. Then she's reaching out with one hand. She's reaching for the balaclava on my head, and I know she wants to grab it and yank it off.

So I pull back—fast.

I put on The Voice.

I say, "This isn't a game."

And the old man says, "It sure as hell isn't." Then he says, "Who the hell is Leon?"

I think, This is all wrong.

First of all, even though I'm still holding a gun, no one seems to be afraid of me anymore.

Second, the old man is also holding a gun. It's pointed right at my head, and I know he's not going to back down. It's what they call a Mexican standoff. It's down to either who will shoot first (*Nobody!* my brain screams. There isn't going to be any shooting!) or who will back down first. I'm tempted to cave. But after coming so far, I can't make myself be the guy who blinks first.

Third, the other guy is staring at me, and I know that he knows without a doubt that it's me under the balaclava. I don't know how he knows, but he knows. Which pretty much wrecks what's left of my plan.

Finally, the girl is frowning, like she hasn't figured out why I'm doing what I'm doing, like the only explanation she can come up with is that I've gone off the deep end. Why else would I be robbing her father's store? And what really throws me is she actually seems to care about it.

Then, just when I think things can't possibly get any worse, a bell sounds behind me. It takes a second before I realize what it means.

It means someone else has come into the store.

Chapter Eleven

Rosie

Daniel is staring at the guy in the mask behind me. He's staring like he thinks if he concentrates hard enough, he'll be able to see through the mask.

Then, out of the corner of my eye, I catch movement, and I see that my dad doesn't have both hands up in the air anymore. Somehow he's managed to edge sideways just enough that he's standing right behind Daniel. He lowers one hand. He's looking at the guy in the mask as he bends ever so slightly to reach under the counter. What is he doing?

His hand re-emerges. It's wrapped around a gun.

A gun!

Where did it come from? I've never seen a gun in the store before. Is it new? There's been a rash of robberies lately. The cops say it's because of all the drugs in the neighborhood, which is a relatively new thing. My dad has been complaining about it, about all the stickups and how the only thing that ever happens is that insurance rates go up for the storeowners.

"They get robbed twice," he says. "First by the punks and the junkies and then by the insurance companies. And you know what? Neither of those two parties understands the concept of an honest day's work."

Or has the gun been there all along? Not that it matters. It's out now, and my father's hand is remarkably steady as he holds it so that it's aimed at the man in the mask behind me.

I know the masked man has seen the gun, because he flinches. His hand tightens on my arm. My heart slams to a stop. Someone is going to get hurt, and it could be me. I'm in the middle between two men who are pointing guns at each other.

Then Daniel says, "Leon?"

I can't help myself. I spin around, a bunch of different thoughts colliding in my head. Leon, telling me he wanted to come and see me tonight. Leon, frowning whenever I tell him I can't go out on account of my father and how strict he is, how mean he is, what a temper he has. Leon, feeling sorry for me and telling me he would do anything for me—anything. The rumors I've heard about Leon's family—especially about Leon's father, which is what gave me the idea in the first place. The surprise I felt when the man in the mask grabbed my arm—how loose his grip was, almost gentle. The masked man's funny voice, weird, unnaturally deep, like he's hiding something. I suddenly realize: like he's hiding his real voice.

I have to know.

I turn my back on the gun in my father's hand and face the gun the man in the mask is holding. But I don't look at it. Instead, I look at the eyes peeking out from the eyeholes. They're hazel, like Leon's eyes, with tiny flecks of green in them, also like Leon's eyes. Around them are stubby brown lashes, just like Leon's.

I look at the mouth that's visible in the mouth hole, but it's harder to notice anything special about it. Then I reach out my hand. I'm sure it's Leon—

sure enough that I plan to pull off the mask and prove it to myself. He watches me. He sees my hand reach out. He jumps back far enough that I can't touch him.

That's when the bell above the door jangles.

That's when Corey walks in.

He doesn't notice anything strange at first because he isn't looking at my father or at the man in the mask. I don't think he even notices the mask. No, he's looking at me, and his face is flushed. I can tell that he's angry—when Corey is angry, he doesn't hide it.

"What's taking so long?" he demands. "I'm up there all by myself, waiting and waiting. You think I have nothing better to do? And why did you lock that door? I had to come around the long way. You think—?"

He stops. He frowns. He looks at my dad, who is scowling at him. He sees the gun in my dad's hand. He glances at me for a split second, like he's expecting me to explain. But I don't have to because his eyes have already moved past me to the man in the mask. The color drains from Corey's face. I guess he doesn't know what else to do because he puts his hands up in the air.

The man in the mask says, "What does he mean he was waiting for you?" This time he sounds exactly like Leon.

Chapter Twelve

Daniel

I can't believe it. The masked man is Leon. Leon Butler, my next-door neighbor, one year ahead of me in school. The quiet one, his mother calls him.

Of her three sons, Leon is the calmest, the most thoughtful. He's the one who, when his mother broke her arm (or, rather, when Leon's father broke his mom's arm), went on the Internet and found a site that showed how to fold laundry properly to avoid wrinkles and then, for the next two months, folded stuff and put it away for his mother. The only one who cooked during those two months. The most the other two did was nuke what was already in the freezer or, failing that, bring home take-out food, always careful to eat when their father was not around. They were always happy to let Leon put the meal on the table and to have things thrown at him if his dad didn't happen to like it.

Leon vacuumed and wiped down the counters and put away the clean dishes from the dishwasher too, rushing home from school to do it and telling his dad that his mother had done it because if there was one thing his dad hated, it was a woman who sat around all day and didn't keep her house in order.

Leon was also the one who, when push finally came to shove, arranged for someone from a shelter to come when his father was at work and take him and his mother and his brothers away someplace where his dad wouldn't find them. His dad never did either. It helped that he was killed in a car crash a week after they left. His blood-alcohol level was through the roof.

The man in the mask is Leon, the non-athletic brother. The one who took piano lessons—although he was never allowed to practice when his dad was in the house—and who excelled at art. The one who actually liked poetry.

Leon, his mother's sweetie (her word, not mine), was wearing a mask and holding a gun and sticking up Mr. Mirelli's store even though, for the past six weeks, he had been going out with Mr. Mirelli's daughter Rosie. What would his mother call him if she knew about that?

He's staring at Rosie, although he keeps glancing at Mr. Mirelli and at Corey Dubuque, who has just stumbled into the store and is mad at Rosie. They used to go together—tough-guy Corey and drop-dead-gorgeous stuck-up Ice Princess Rosie—but, boy, he didn't make it easy for her.

Corey's problem: he has a temper. But, despite everything, he somehow got himself recognized as cool. Guys like to hang out with Corey. Girls like to dream about being with him.

Personally, I don't understand it. Yeah, I can see that he's not bad-looking. Yeah, I get that his sarcasm and back talking to teachers are big hits, because Corey steps up and says stuff the rest of us only dream about saying. And, yeah, I can see the appeal of knowing someone who's as connected as Corey is. No matter what you need—

party invites, fake IDs, booze, smokes, you name it—Corey can get it. And besides that wicked mean temper of his, he has a sense of humor and a quick wit. You figure a guy who makes you laugh until you feel like your sides are going to split open can't be that bad.

But I'll tell you what—he doesn't look so cute and so cool standing there between two guns with his hands so high you'd swear he was trying to grab hold of the ceiling so he can pull himself up out of harm's way.

And Leon doesn't seem so sweet as he turns, the gun turning with him, so he can get a good long look at Corey.

"Leon," Rosie says sharply, sounding like her old self now. "Put that gun down right this second."

"Leon?" Corey says, confused. He's looking at Rosie, trying to match up the words she's speaking with the scene he sees in front of his eyes.

"What does he mean, Rosie?" Leon says. "Why was he waiting for you?"

"Put the gun down, Leon," Rosie says.

"Leon the Loser?" Corey asks.

Rosie nods, but in a distracted way.

"Yeah, Leon. Put the gun down," Corey says, cocky now that he knows who he's dealing with.

I guess no one told him you can catch more flies with honey than you can with vinegar. I guess no one told him that even though a doofus with a gun might still be a doofus, the fact that he's armed makes him dangerous. I guess it never occurred to Corey that it takes an even bigger doofus to piss off a man with a gun.

Leon doesn't put the gun down. "What does he mean, Rosie? Why was he waiting for you?" he says. He doesn't sound sweet either. He sounds confused. He also sounds impatient: how many times does he have to ask before he gets an answer?

"Leon, please put the gun down," Rosie says, the nervousness in her voice matching the impatience in his. Maybe I'm wrong, but I'm getting the feeling that she doesn't want to answer Leon's question while Leon is holding a gun because she suspects—maybe she even knows for a fact—that he isn't going to like what she says.

Leon isn't the only one who is impatient. Mr. Mirelli is too. "Rosie," he says. "Do you know this clown?"

"Please, Leon?" She's begging him now. "Put the gun down."

"Yeah, idiot," Corey says, taking a step toward him. "Put the gun down." He's halfway to Leon, his hand out to grab the gun, when Leon aims it directly at him and braces himself, like he's ready to shoot.

"Leon!" Rosie is frantic. Her voice is shrill.

"Leon." It's Mr. Mirelli now. "Leon, look at me."

Leon doesn't look, but I do. Mr. Mirelli's gun is pointed at him.

"Why was he waiting for you, Rosie?" Leon says. "He treated you like garbage. He used you, and then he just threw you aside."

"What?" Corey says. His face is flushed. He looks angry.

"What?" Mr. Mirelli says at exactly the same time.

Rosie holds her arms away from her sides. Her whole body seems to be saying, *I'm no threat to you, Leon. I'm not going to hurt you.*

But it turns out you don't need a gun to hurt someone.

"You're a good person, Leon," Rosie says in a soft voice. "I don't know what

I would have done without you. You were there for me, and I'll never forget that."

Leon is shaking his head. He knows, the same as I do, what she really means. He knows exactly where this is going.

"Corey came back," Rosie says. She takes another half-step closer to Leon. "Corey came back. He loves me, Leon." She smiles at him, and it's the expression of an angel. All of a sudden I understand why Leon has been following her around like a puppy for the last six weeks. A guy like Leon, a sensitive guy, his mother's sweetie, who has never been with a girl before, a guy like that could never resist that smile.

"*I* love you," Leon says. "That's why I'm here."

I hear an explosion of laughter. It's Corey.

"Right," he says. "Nothing says love better than a gun and a mask."

Leon's eyes harden in the eyeholes of the balaclava. His lips twist.

"For the love of God," Mr. Mirelli says, disgusted. "You, Leon, put that gun away and get the hell out of my store before I call the cops." I bet he'll call the cops anyway. "And you." His eyes flick to Corey. "Go away. Rosie's not going anywhere with you. She's busy."

"Corey's not leaving," Rosie says. She reaches for his hand, and he takes hers. "Not without me."

Chapter Thirteen

The Masked Man

Rosie isn't listening to me. She isn't looking at me either. She's looking at Corey.

"You said you wanted out," I tell her. Just like my mom wanted out. "You said he practically keeps you a prisoner." Just like my dad kept my mom a prisoner. "That's why I'm here. To get you out." Like I got my mother out.

"Who keeps you a prisoner?" Mr. Mirelli says, all surprised, like he has no idea what I'm talking about. He reminds me of my dad talking to the cops that one time I called them: *Hurt my wife? Officer, I would never hurt my wife. I love her.* But he hurt her bad as soon as the cops left. Then he hurt me.

"You do," I tell Mr. Mirelli. "You keep her a prisoner. But you're not going to get away with that anymore. I'm not going to let you."

"Get away with what?" He looks at Rosie. "What's he talking about?"

They're all like that. My father was like that. He used to yell at my mother all the time. He used to tell her she was ugly (she isn't) and stupid (she isn't) and worthless (he was the worthless one). He used to hit her, usually in places where no one would see it. But sometimes he got extra wound up. Sometimes he hit her in the face. Then he'd tell her,

"You say one word and you'll be sorry." So she would either stay in the house until the bruises were gone or she'd make up some excuse, like she fell. And people would go along with it. That's what really killed me. People would go along with whatever she said, like they didn't care.

Well, I cared. And I did something.

First, I took away my dad's gun, and I didn't let his threats and beatings force me to admit it was me. Then I called a shelter and arranged to get us all out of there. I don't know what I was going to do with the gun. I told myself I took it to make sure that he didn't decide to use it. But, really, it felt good having it in case he found us after we left the shelter, in case he threatened my mother again, in case he beat her again. I didn't have anything to do with what happened to my dad after that. Nobody made him drive drunk. But am I sorry he's gone? No way.

I didn't turn my back on my mom like everyone else did. And I wasn't going to turn my back on Rosie.

"That's why I'm here, Rosie," I say. "To take you away."

"*You're* here to take her away?" Corey says. He glares at Rosie. "What the hell is going on?"

"Don't you talk to my daughter like that," Mr. Mirelli shouts at him.

"It's okay," Rosie tells Corey. "Just give me a minute."

"Give me a minute. Give me ten minutes. I'll be right back, I promise." Corey says all of this in a phoney girl voice. He's making fun of Rosie.

I try to shut him out. I try to shut out Mr. Mirelli too. I focus on Rosie.

"We can go," I tell her. "We can go right now."

She's shaking her head.

"You don't have to put up with him anymore, Rosie. You don't have to let him hit you or bully you anymore."

"Hit you?" Mr. Mirelli says. "Did someone hit you, Rosie?"

"You know *someone* did," I yell at him. He's just like my father, with that stupid "Who, me?" expression on his face, like he doesn't have a clue what I'm talking about. I struggle to get a grip. I tell myself that it isn't about him. It's about Rosie. "I thought—Rosie, you said you wanted to run away somewhere where he would never find you."

I've seen it on TV a dozen times. A guy in a mask walks into a store. He sticks up the place and takes off with the owner's daughter. He tells the owner, *Don't even think about calling the cops.* He trusts that the man won't, at least not for a while. By the time the man does make the call, the man in the mask is long gone. So is the girl.

That was my plan. Get Rosie safely away from her old man and then meet up with her later when the coast is clear. The cops would think that some man with a gun took her and maybe killed her or something. They would look, but they wouldn't find her. Neither would her father. She would be free—and no one would ever suspect I had anything to do with it. At least, they wouldn't have if Daniel hadn't been in the store.

Rosie says, "I can't go with you, Leon."

Can't go? My mother used to say that. She said it because she was afraid.

"Yes, you can," I tell her. "I have it all worked out. You'll be safe. He'll never find you."

She's shaking her head again. "I can't."

"But you said...Rosie, what about the baby?"

"Baby?" Mr. Mirelli says.

"Baby?" Corey says at exactly the same time.

The baby. From that one time Rosie and I were together. From the time she cried and cried, and I put my arms around her. I didn't know what else to do. I put my arms around her and I held her. I told her everything was going to be okay. The next thing I knew, we were kissing. It was only the one time, but it changed everything. That's why I'm here.

Chapter Fourteen

Rosie

Everyone is staring at me.

"What baby?" my father is yelling. I wish he didn't have that gun in his hand.

"Yeah," Corey says. "What baby?"

"Our baby," Leon says.

Corey is staring at me. I know what he's thinking. He's wondering how much I could have loved him if I went off and got myself pregnant with another guy—worse, with a guy like Leon. He doesn't understand. How could he?

I was with Corey forever—the whole year. I loved him. I *love* him. I don't think I could ever love anyone who wasn't Corey. But he fooled around with that other girl, and we got into a fight over it. I was the one who started it, even though I knew Corey well enough that I could have—should have—predicted exactly what he would do. Which turned out to be exactly what he did. He dumped me. He took off up to his uncle's place. He wouldn't return my calls. Two days after he left, I found out I was pregnant.

I could have gone to a clinic. They would have helped me. But it's Corey's baby. How could I get rid of Corey's baby?

Of course my dad would have freaked out if I told him. Look at him now, red-faced, scowling, looking like he wants to shoot Leon more now than he did when all Leon was doing was robbing the store, which, it turns out, he really isn't doing at all.

Leon's a nice guy. Sweet. Not a boyfriend kind of guy—not for me anyway—but a friend kind of guy. He caught me crying at my locker after I found out about the baby. He crept up to me like I was a bunny with its foot caught in a snare and he was a kind hunter who was going to set me free. When he asked me what was wrong, I started to sob. I couldn't make myself tell him what Corey had done.

He drove me home. He watched out for me the next day and the day after that. He brought me a teddy bear to cheer me up. He knew I was crying about Corey, but he never mentioned his name because he didn't want to remind me. He didn't know about the baby. He didn't know how scared I was to have a baby by myself or how much more scared I was of what my dad would do if he found out.

Then I had an idea.

I let him do it with me—just once. When I finally told him I was pregnant, he assumed the baby was his. I figured my dad wouldn't push me so hard to get rid of it if the guy was still in the picture. I could keep the baby, and then later, when Corey came back—I knew he would eventually—there I'd be, with his baby. He would take me back. We would be a family.

But Corey wasn't supposed to find out like this. He wasn't supposed to be hearing about his baby for the first time from Leon.

"It's not *our* baby, Leon," I say. "It's *my* baby."

I see confusion in Leon's eyes. And Corey's.

"What do you mean, *your* baby?" Corey says. There's a tremble in his voice.

"*What baby*?" my dad yells.

"It's your baby, Corey." I move toward him and take his hands in mine. "Yours and mine."

Behind me, Leon says, "Liar. It's *my* baby."

I'm staring into Corey's eyes, trying to make him see that I'm telling the truth. He has a little-boy face now—full of fear and wonder. At least, I think that's what I'm seeing.

"A baby?" he says, as if he can hardly believe what I'm telling him.

I nod. "Our baby."

"Liar!" Leon says again.

"Shut up, dickhead," Corey yells at him. "She's not talking to you. She's talking to me."

"Pregnant?" my dad says. "You got yourself pregnant?"

"It's mine," Leon says. "Don't be afraid, Rosie. Tell him the truth. Tell him about us."

"I told you to shut up," Corey growls. "Like she would ever touch you."

"She did. She and I—"

"Shut up, Leon," I say. He's going to ruin everything. "I already told you—it's not yours."

"But you said—"

"I said it because of him." I nod at my father. "He would have made me get rid of it if there wasn't a father."

Even with a mask on, Leon manages to look crushed. His eyes are watery. His mouth droops. I can't help feeling sorry for him. He's a nice guy.

Corey's expression is different. His eyes are hard now. So is his mouth. He says, "Why would he think the baby is his, Rosie? I don't believe in immaculate conception, not for you. So what did you do to make him think it's his baby, huh? What did you do?"

Chapter Fifteen

Daniel

I'm out of it now. I back up a full pace. No one notices me. Corey is too busy screaming at Rosie. Rosie is too busy telling him it's not what he thinks, that she was only trying to protect the baby, that there was no way her dad would have let her take on some guy's baby all by herself, no way. She tells him,

"I love you, Corey. I always loved you. I'll never love anyone else."

"He didn't protect you," Leon says. "He didn't even try. He ran out on you."

"He came back," Rosie tells him. There's a sharpness to her tone, like she wishes he would go away.

"Yeah, well, where was he when your dad was keeping you a prisoner?"

"Prisoner?" Mr. Mirelli says. "What is he talking about, Rosie? When did I ever keep you a prisoner?"

"It's nothing, Daddy. He doesn't know what he's talking about."

"Why are you saying that?" Leon asks. "Because you're afraid of him? You don't have to be afraid anymore, Rosie. I won't let him hurt you."

"Hurt her?" Mr. Mirelli says. "I would never hurt my daughter."

"Says you," Leon shoots back. "She told me all about it. She told me how you keep her locked up here and how you beat her when she disobeys you."

"Beat her?" The old man looks at Rosie. "What is he talking about? When did I ever beat you?"

"It's okay, Daddy." She turns to Leon. "It's not true. What I said about my dad, I only said it because you never take no for an answer." She twists her head a little so that now she's talking to Corey. "He never left me alone. He wanted to be with me all the time. I had to tell him something to make him stop bothering me."

"I wanted to protect you," Leon says. "You told me—"

Rosie's eyes freeze over like a pond in January. "I told you so that you'd leave me alone. I don't love you, Leon. It's not your baby."

"Then why does he think it is?" Corey asks again. "Guys don't think they got a girl pregnant unless they were with that girl, you know what I mean, Rosie?"

"It was just one time, I swear. It's our baby, Corey. Yours and mine."

Corey's eyes narrow. "How do I know that? Because you say so? You told him it was his. How do I know it isn't? How do I know you're not lying to me?"

"I would never lie to you, Corey." She reaches for his hand again, but he pulls back from her.

"When were you going to tell me?"

"You wouldn't answer my calls," Rosie says.

"I don't even want a kid," he says. "Kids tie you down. I'm too young to be tied down."

"But it's ours. You'll love it. You'll see. Guys are always nervous at first, aren't they, Daddy?" She looks anxiously at her father, whom she has been spreading lies about. "But it's okay. Isn't it, Daddy? Tell him."

Her father stares stonily at her. He doesn't say a word.

"You want a baby, be my guest," Corey says. "But I don't want anything to do with it. You thought you could trap me. Well, you're wrong." He turns away from her.

"Corey." She's practically hysterical now. "Corey, please!"

"You see?" Leon says. "He's no good. He doesn't care. But I do. I don't care if it's not my baby. It's yours. That's good enough for me. I'll look after you, Rosie."

Rosie swings around to face him, her hands clenched at her sides, her pretty face a knot of anger.

"Go away, Leon," she screams at him. "Just go away. Get out of my life!"

"But, Rosie, I love you."

The poor dumb schmuck. Maybe his mother thinks he's sweet. But if you ask me, he's not too bright, not to mention he's both blind and deaf.

"I hate you!" Rosie screams at him.

"I'm out of here," Corey says.

"No!" Rosie lunges for him. "No, Corey. Wait, please don't go." She grabs one of his arms and holds tight. "Don't go. I'm packed. Please—"

"Packed?" Mr. Mirelli says. I'm starting to feel sorry for him. Surprises keep dropping on him like bombs. "What do you mean packed? Where are you going? What's happened, Rosie? We can talk about it. Whatever it is, we can talk about it."

But Rosie isn't paying any attention to her father. She's hanging on to Corey, and Corey is trying to shake her off. Rosie won't let go. She's crying and begging and holding on so that he has to drag her with him with every step he takes.

"Corey, listen to me—"

But Corey and his temper don't want to listen. They want out. Corey pries her hands off his arm, bending her fingers back so far that she lets out a howl. Mr. Mirelli lifts the panel in the counter so that he can go to her. But before he can slip through the opening, Corey has unlatched her fingers from his arm and has shoved her so hard that she flies backward away from him. She doesn't stop until she hits the ground and her head cracks against the edge of an ice-cream freezer. We all stare at her. We're probably all doing what I'm doing, which is trying to see if her chest is moving, if she's breathing. But I can't tell.

Mr. Mirelli runs to her and kneels down. He says, "Someone call an ambulance." His face is white as he bends to feel for a pulse.

I pull out my cell phone and make the call. Out of the corner of my eye, I see Corey dart for the door. Then I hear a bang, louder than anything I've ever heard before, and Corey crumples.

Leon stands there for a moment, the gun still out in front of him. It seems to take forever for him to lower it. He pulls the mask off his head. His eyes are red. His face is wet, maybe from tears or maybe from sweat. He doesn't even try to run.

"I was going to look after her," he says, his voice as limp as his hair. "I was going to take care of her and the baby. He was only going to hurt the baby. Why do they always go for the ones who hurt them?"

He's not looking at me when he asks it. He's looking at Corey. So I keep my mouth shut. I mean, he's still holding that gun, and if I didn't know it before, I know it now—it's loaded.

Leon is still standing in the exact same place when the police and the ambulance arrive.

The cops see the gun in his hand and out come their guns. They're yelling at him, "Put the gun down! Put the gun down!" When he stoops and lays it on the ground, one of them grabs it. Then they yell at him to get face down on the floor. Suddenly they're all over him, handcuffing him, reading him his rights, getting him out of the store and into a cop car.

Meanwhile the ambulance crew has split up. One guy is checking out Rosie. The other is on Corey. As far as I can tell, they're both still alive. It's harder to figure out from what the ambulance guys are saying how badly hurt they are. A second ambulance arrives. There's a lot of activity. Then Rosie and Corey are bundled into the ambulances and whisked to the hospital. Mr. Mirelli wants to go with Rosie, but the cops won't let him, not yet, not until they ask him a few questions. They ask hundreds of them, to both him and me. They ask the same ones over and over. My brain feels like it's going to shut down long before they finish.

Chapter Sixteen

Daniel

Rosie lost her baby. She was off school for a long time. Today is her first day back. She doesn't look like she used to. If she's wearing any makeup, it's not the kind you'd notice. It's weird, but she looks even prettier now than she did before, even though she's thinner and paler and doesn't work at being the center of attention. In fact, she's superquiet.

Corey lost the use of his right arm. He never came back to school. If Rosie ever saw him again, she kept it to herself.

Leon was arrested on a bunch of charges. His mother tried to get Mr. Mirelli to drop the ones relating to the attempted robbery, but he refused. She tried to get Leon out on bail, too, but that didn't work out either. His mom told my mom that he believed Rosie when she told him about her father and that, given what he experienced with his own dad, he just wanted to save her. But he went about it the wrong way. Maybe he was trying to do something good. But the fact is, he scared everyone to death. And he shot Corey.

I'm sitting in the cafeteria the day Rosie comes back to school. I have a mystery-shopper assignment scheduled for after school, and I'm looking over my checklist to see what I have to report on. A shadow falls across my table.

It's Rosie.

She's holding an apple and a container of skimmed milk. She says, "Is it okay if I sit with you, Daniel?"

I guess I stare stupidly at her. I'm too surprised to say anything.

"If you don't want me to—," she begins.

"No. It's fine." I jump up and pull out a chair for her. She sits down and puts her apple and her container of milk on the table in front of her.

"My dad sold the store," she says.

I already know.

"He held out for a good price."

I know that too. It turns out he's a good negotiator. He got more than my uncle's friend wanted to pay.

"He says he wants to spend more time with me. We're going away for the summer, just the two of us."

She opens her milk and slips a straw in. For a moment, it looks like she's going to smile, but she doesn't. She takes a sip of milk and says, "So, what are you working on?" It sounds like she really cares.

Norah McClintock has written numerous novels, including *Marked*, *Bang* and *Snitch*. Norah lives in Toronto, Ontario.

orca soundings

The following is an excerpt from another exciting Orca Soundings novel, *Knifepoint* by Alex Van Tol.

978-1-55469-305-4 $9.95 pb
978-1-55469-306-1 $16.95 lib

JILL TOOK A JOB THAT SOUNDED PERFECT for the summer, guiding tourists on trail rides in the beautiful mountains. She didn't realize that the money was terrible, the hours long and the co-workers insufferable. After a blow-up with her boss, she takes a lone man into the mountains for a ride, only to find that he is a dangerous killer. When Jill fights back and manages to escape, she is in a desperate race to survive and make it to safety.

Chapter One

Voices, sudden and loud, jolt me out of my dream. Confused, I try to sit up. But I can't. It feels like I've been tied to the bed with a million tiny threads. I force one eye open. Turn my head. The clock radio says *6:44*. The voices keep shouting. They're coming from the radio. The same radio I've woken up to for the past thirty-five days, at the same ungodly hour.

Except every morning it gets harder.

I raise my head and look at the wooden walls. A million tiny daggers shoot through my skull. Ugh. I prop myself on one elbow and hit *Snooze*. The daggers turn into hammers and spread out across my body. About a thousand go to work on the soles of my feet. I swing my feet out of bed, careful not to touch them to the floor. I can't face that agony yet. Yawning, I reach for some socks. I've *got* to start going to bed earlier. I can't keep functioning on five hours of sleep a night. Not when my job beats the crap out of me every day.

The metal bedframe squeaks as I heave myself up. Owww, ow. I could die right about now. If a serial killer poked his head into my room and offered to stab me at this exact moment,

I'd tell him to go right ahead. I wonder if it's normal for my feet to hurt this much.

Well, yeah, maybe. When you spend fourteen hours working and then another five dancing nonstop. But it's so fun!

I glance at the clock again. *6:53.* I shove my screaming feet into my cowboy boots. I look at them. They're filthy, caked in horseshit after the July rains. I'm not supposed to wear them inside the bunkhouse, but whatever. I can't scrub the crap off either. I've tried. It's all over the bottom of my chaps too. That's a bummer. I spent a lot to have those custom made. That was back when I thought I'd be making $12.50 an hour.

Back before I found out that what James really meant was $1250 *a month.*

Slave labor, that's what it is. Kristi and I calculated it a few weeks ago—a couple of days before she ditched the ranch to go find a decent-paying job in the city. Turns out I make about $4.46 an hour. It's *hard* work, too, being a wrangler: chucking hay bales, hefting saddles, dragging buckets of grain, pushing and pulling around 1500-pound animals all day long.

Thinking of the horses gets me moving. The first barn shift starts at seven, and being late sucks. If you start your morning late, you spend all day playing catch-up.

I leave the rest of the bunkhouse sleeping, closing the door softly behind me.

The cold morning air stings my throat as I hobble across the grass to the main lodge. My feet are killing me. Heavy dew darkens my boots. God, it feels like winter's coming already. I shiver, wishing I'd dug around to find my gloves.

I push open the screen door leading to the kitchen. Steve, the morning cook, hands me a muffin on my way through. He's nice enough but looks like he just escaped maximum-security prison. Who knows, maybe he did. They're not particularly strict with their hiring practices around here. Steve has so many tattoos it's hard to see any un-inked flesh on his arms. I like him though. He feeds me for free. The other cooks make you punch a meal card if you want so much as a package of saltines.

"You look like shit, Jill," he says pleasantly.

"Kiss my chaps, kitchen boy," I snarl over my shoulder.

Steve laughs, then growls at me. "With pleasure."

Pit stop at the coffee machine. Then straight out to the barn. Hopefully there won't be a nine o'clock ride. If there isn't, I'll be able to come back into the restaurant and eat a proper breakfast after I get the horses saddled.

No one's at the barn when I get there. I figured as much. Carrie and Laura downed a whole lot of beer last night. It's not the first time they haven't shown up for their shift. And I'm certain it won't be the last either. They get away with murder, those two. Jerks. If *I* ever overslept and missed the start of my shift, I'd sure as hell hear about it. But they're the queen bees, so I keep my head down and my mouth shut.

Whiskey snorts in recognition when she sees me. I give her a quick brush, pitch a blanket and saddle onto her back and sling a bridle over her soft face.

Where's Kim? I'd almost be glad to see her grumpy butt marching around the corral this morning, swearing at random horses and kicking any that looked at her the wrong way. She's a total cow. But I gotta say, she gets stuff done around the barn. If she was here, she'd have dragged Carrie and Laura out of bed by their long sexy hair. She's the only one who'd dare.

Now I remember. It's Kim's day off. Damn. No Kim, no Carrie, no Laura. No one else on the schedule. I'll have to round up the horses on my own.

All sixty of them.

I swallow my butterflies and swing up onto Whiskey's back. I turn her head toward the night pasture.

I have no idea whether I'll be able to gather up five dozen horses and herd them in one tidy bunch toward the barn. I'm not a born-and-raised cowhand by any stretch. As far as I know, nobody has ever rounded up on their own. Lucky me. But what else can I do? I can't wait until one of the beautiful drunkards staggers in for her shift. That could be hours. By then there'll be guests lined up along the corral fences, waiting for their trail rides.

I've got to do it.

When we get there, Whiskey and I run a quick perimeter check around the night pasture. I crack the whip and get them all moving toward the gate.

I wait until every horse is crammed up against the fence, noses, necks and bums all crowded together in a warm shifting mass. Whiskey and I wedge our way along the fence to the gate. I hold my breath and flip the latch off the gatepost. The gate groans open, powered by a dozen hungry horses.

I crack the whip. "Hyaaaaagh! *Let's go, boys!*"

Startled, the horses bolt straight out of the gate and pound along the road leading to the barn.

Right on. *Go, Jill!* I give Whiskey a kick and we lurch away, chasing the heels of the horses at the back. "Hyaaagh!" Over and over I shout and crack the whip. The horses thunder along the road, kicking up dust in the morning sunlight. They hammer into the main corral and spread out along the fences, content to be hemmed in again. I close the corral gate behind them and slide to the ground, surprised that my shaking knees hold me up.

"Nice work," says an appreciative voice. I spin around. A guy I don't recognize is leaning against the fence. He's maybe in his mid-twenties. Dark hair. Red shirt. He flashes a grin at me. *Oh.* And he's gorgeous. Was he watching that whole time? I feel myself flush. Stupid.

"Thanks." I can't think of anything else to say, so I tie Whiskey to a fencepost and loosen her saddle. I jerk a halter off a peg and walk out into the corral. I slide it over Ace's head and lead him into the barn. I grab another halter.

"I'm Darren Parker. From Bar G," he says. His voice is friendly. I know that ranch. It's just up the valley, about twenty minutes away. "You guys do adventure rides?"

I swallow. An adventure ride? Yeah, we do them. But I sure hope that's not what he's after. A trail ride is one thing. The horses just line up and follow each other's butts through the forest for a couple of hours. But adventure rides? Crashing through rivers, pelting down hills and racing through meadows? I hate taking out adventure rides.

Don't get me wrong. I love running my horse fast and taking crazy chances. But I don't like being responsible for other people during a fast, risky ride. I don't have the same kind of horse background that the other wranglers have.

Nope, adventure rides aren't my thing. It's hard enough for me to hang on to my own damn horse, let alone look after someone else's.

But I don't say any of this. Maybe this guy will be able to handle himself. Being a wrangler and all.

"Rides start at nine o'clock." I glance at him. "You might as well go in and have breakfast while you wait."

With that, I turn back to the work of catching horses. And I hope to hell that he can't hear my heart as it tries to pound its way through my chest.

orca soundings

For more information on all the books in the Orca Soundings series, please visit **www.orcabook.com.**